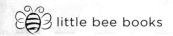

An imprint of Bonnier Publishing Group
853 Broadway, New York, New York 10003
Copyright © 2015 by Igloo Books Ltd
This little bee books edition, 2016.
All rights reserved, including the right of
reproduction in whole or in part in any form.
LITTLE BEE BOOKS is a trademark of
Bonnier Publishing Group, and
associated colophon is a trademark of
Bonnier Publishing Group.

Manufactured in China HUN001 0915
First Edition 2 4 6 8 10 9 7 5 3 1
Library of Congress Cataloging-in-
Publication Data is available upon request.
ISBN 978-1-4998-0212-2

littlebeebooks.com
bonnierpublishing.com

I Love You
Because...

little bee books

You look so cute in the morning, all snuggled up in bed,
as sunbeams shine on you, my little sleepyhead.

It makes me feel so happy when you say,
"Mommy, I love you."
Now, I'll tell you all the reasons why
I love you, too.

Sometimes you are
very bouncy and love
to jump around.

"Watch me, Mommy!"
you cry, as you roll
on the ground.

We play hide-and-seek and
splash in puddles, too.

You love to squeal and run away
when I chase after you.

I love you because you want to play, no matter what the weather.

You giggle with your little friends, as you have fun together.

I love you because you say my stories
are the best you've ever heard.

You sit very still, without a sound,
listening to every word.

You give me lovely hugs,
which are cuddly and
as warm as toast.

Your tickly kisses make
me giggle, and I love
them the most.

I love you because you are very brave,
even when you cry.
I dab at your dribbly, trickly tears and
gently wipe them dry.

Sometimes we sit together
in the evening light.
We watch the pale moon rise,
waiting for the night.

You are the most precious thing to me.
There is no one quite like you.
I know you will always love me, and
I will always love you, too.

I love you,

Little Bunny.